JACK A
THE BEANSTALK

Illustrations by Gabhor Utomo

APPLESAUCE PRESS

13-Digit ISBN: 978-1-64643-184-7
10-Digit ISBN: 1-64643-184-7

This book may be ordered by mail from the publisher.
Please include $5.95 for postage and handling.
Please support your local bookseller first!

Books published by Cider Mill Press Book Publishers are available at special discounts for
bulk purchases in the United States by corporations, institutions, and other organizations.
For more information, please contact the publisher.

Applesauce Press is an imprint of
Cider Mill Press Book Publishers
"Where Good Books Are Ready for Press"
501 Nelson Place
Nashville, Tennessee 37214

cidermillpress.com

Typography: ITC Caslon 224
Printed in China

23 24 25 26 27 DSC 7 6 5 4 3

O nce upon a time, there lived a poor widow and her son Jack. All they had to live on was the milk that their cow, Milky-White, gave every morning. But one morning Milky-White gave no milk, and they didn't know what to do. Jack's mother told him to sell the cow.

So Jack went to the market and on the way he met a strange man who wanted to buy his cow.

Jack asked, "What will you give me in return for my cow?"

The peculiar man answered, "I will give you five magic beans!" Jack took the magic beans and gave the man the cow.

But when he reached home, Jack's mother was
very angry. She cried, "You fool! He took our cow
and gave you some beans!" She threw the beans out
the window. Jack was very sad and went to sleep
without dinner.

When Jack woke up the next morning,
he looked out the window and saw that a huge
beanstalk had grown from his magic beans.

Using the leaves and twisty vines like the rungs of a ladder, Jack climbed and climbed until at last he reached the sky.

When he got to the top, he found a long road winding its way through the clouds to a tall castle off in the distance.

There in the kingdom in the sky lived a giant
and his wife. Jack ran up the road toward the castle,
and just as he reached it, the door swung open to
reveal the giant's wife.

Jack asked, "Could you please give me something to eat? I am so hungry!" The kind wife brought him to the kitchen and gave him some bread and milk.

Jack had only taken a few bites when the whole house began to tremble with the noise of someone coming. *Thump! Thump! Thump!* Then he saw the giant. The giant was very big and looked very fearsome. Jack was terrified, and the wife hid him in a pot just as the giant came inside. The giant cried, "Fee-fi-fo-fum, I smell the blood of a little boy. Be he alive, or be he dead, I'll grind his bones to make my bread!"

The wife replied, "There is no boy in here!"
So the giant ate his food and then went to his room.
He took out his sacks of gold coins, counted them,
and put them aside. Then he went to sleep.

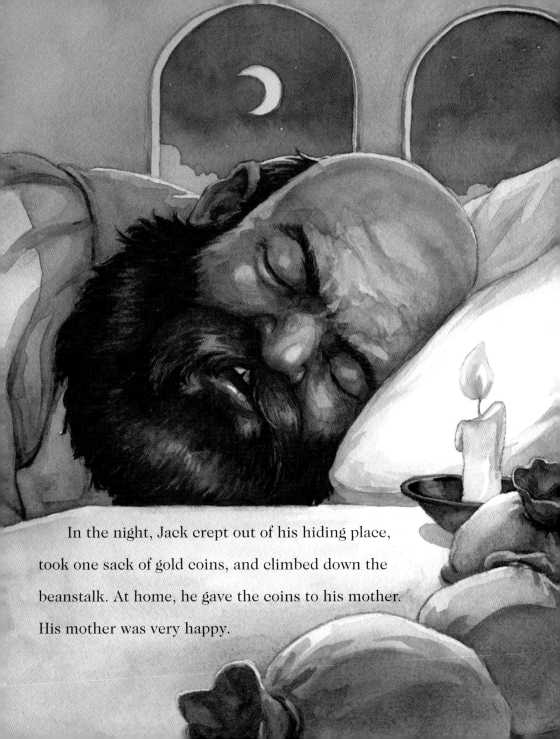

In the night, Jack crept out of his hiding place,
took one sack of gold coins, and climbed down the
beanstalk. At home, he gave the coins to his mother.
His mother was very happy.

The very next day, Jack climbed the beanstalk and went to the giant's house again. Once again, Jack asked the giant's wife for food, but while he was eating the giant returned. *Thump! Thump! Thump!* Jack leapt up in fright and hid under the bed. The giant cried, "Fee-fi-fo-fum, I smell the blood of a little boy. Be he alive, or be he dead, I'll grind his bones to make my bread!"

The wife said, "There is no boy in here!"

So the giant ate his food and went to his room. There, he took out a hen. He shouted, "Lay!" and the hen laid a golden egg. When the giant finally fell asleep and the house shook with his snores, Jack tiptoed out of his hiding place, took the hen, and climbed down the beanstalk. Jack's mother was very happy with him, for the hen would make them rich once more.

After some days, Jack once again climbed the beanstalk and went to the giant's castle. For the third time, Jack met the giant's wife and asked for some food. Once again, the giant's wife gave him bread and milk. But while Jack was eating, the giant came home. *Thump! Thump! Thump!* Jack quickly hid in a wardrobe.

"Fee-fi-fo-fum, I smell the blood of a little boy. Be he alive, or be he dead, I'll grind his bones to make my bread!" cried the giant.

"Don't be silly! There is no boy in here!" said his wife.

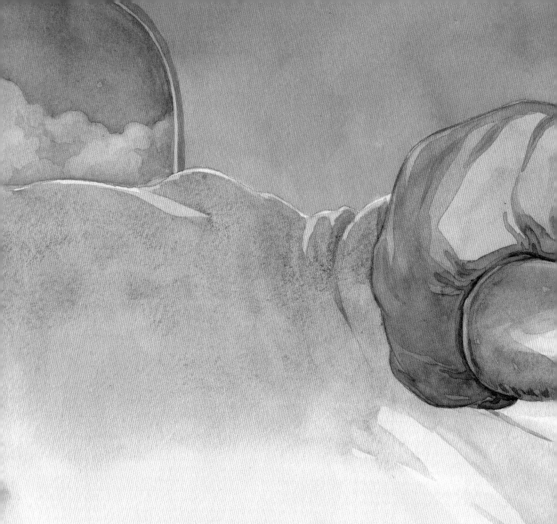

So the giant ate his food and went to his room. The giant took out a magical harp that could play beautiful songs. He shouted, "Sing!" and the harp began to play and lulled the giant to sleep. While the giant slept, Jack snuck out of the wardrobe and grabbed the harp.

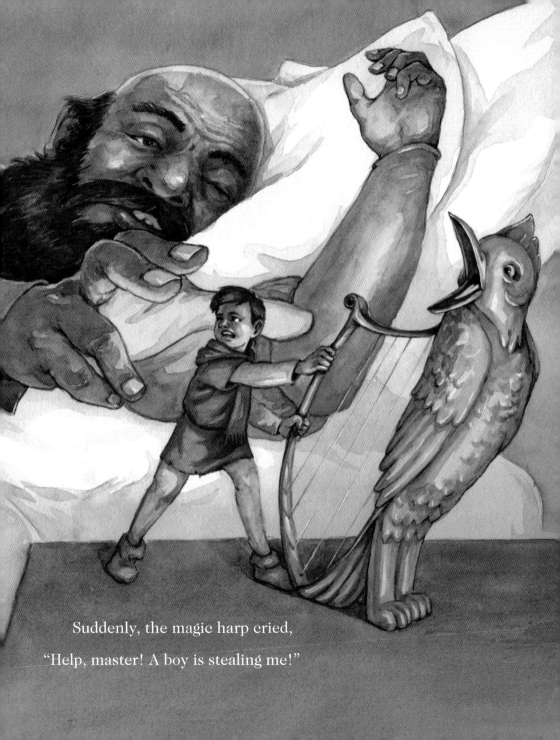

Suddenly, the magic harp cried,

"Help, master! A boy is stealing me!"

The giant woke up and saw Jack with the harp. With a tremendous roar, he sprang from his bed and reached the door in two strides. But Jack was too fast for him. He raced like lightning down the beanstalk and reached home.

As luck would have it, Jack's mother was outside chopping wood. "Mother! Mother!" cried Jack. "Make haste and give me the axe."

His mother ran to him with the hatchet in her hand, and Jack cut through the beanstalk in one tremendous blow. It fell to the ground with a terrible crash. The outraged giant gave a mighty bellow, but he could not reach the ground. Jack and his mother lived happily ever after.

The End

About Applesauce Press

Good ideas ripen with time. From seed to harvest,
Applesauce Press crafts books with beautiful designs, creative
formats, and kid-friendly information on a variety of fascinating topics.
Like our parent company, Cider Mill Press Book Publishers,
our press bears fruit twice a year, publishing
a new crop of titles each spring and fall.

501 Nelson Place
Nashville, Tennessee 37214

cidermillpress.com